This book
belongs to

♥

_____

This book is dedicated to my beautiful daughter Baye (6).

Ever since she entered into my life she has enabled me to really enhance my crazy imagination.

Everyday Baye amazes me with her caring nature - inner strength and her magical creativeness.

This book has every ounce of love it could possibly have in it and I thank my gorgeous girl for being the most inspiring young lady I've ever known.

So Bubba Chop, this book is just for you!
lots of love
Mummy xxxxxx

Look out for
this Star Lizard ;)

ISBN: 9798556030404

Dexxy
The
Determined Dragon!

Author

Gemma Bond ☆☆

Illustrator

Jo Blake

Dexxy the mystical dragon
Is the creature we most admire.
She's always helping her friends
With her dragon's breath of fire.

The lovely Squirrel Family,
Shivering and trying to cope,
See Dexxy walk on over,
And now they are full of hope.

"Oh please Dexxy, light our fire.
It's so awfully cold in here."
As Dexxy blows her giant flame,
She tells them to stand clear!

"Wow, Dexxy, you are the best,
Thank you so much for your care.
You have made our day happy."
There is magic in the air.

Dexxy is now flying.
She sees Wilbur
Scratch his head.
"Hi there, Wilbur.
Are you okay?"
She senses Wilbur's
Dread.

"Hello, Dexxy. I'm not Ok.
My heart's begun to ache,
It's our annual Walrus party,
And we can't light the cake."

Dexxy takes a deep breath in
And blows a lively flame.
"Thank goodness, the candles are lit!
We are so glad you came."

Annual
Walrus
Party

Dexxy is just so happy,
Always there to help her friends.
She really doesn't mind
The amount of time she spends.

Up ahead she notices
Pearl the Polar bear.
She sighs and looks bemused.
Dexxy's nostrils begin to flare.

"Hey, Pearl. What is wrong?"
"Oh Dexxy, my bike is stuck!
I can't untie the rope from it
Today, I have no luck."

This is no problem for Dexxy.
"In a second, I'll burn it free."
Dexxy opens her mouth to breathe fire,
But there's no fire to be seen!

"Hold on, Pearl.
I will try again.
It will work this time
I'm sure."
She gives the biggest
Puff she can,
But her fire is no more!

Instantly, Dexxy's face falls
She walks off with head hanging down.
"I don't understand what's happened."
She gives a discouraged frown.

She slumps against a cold rock,
Tears rolling down her cheeks.
"I can't help my friend at all!"
Her day is looking bleak.

"Dexxy, Dexxy, how are you?"
Says a happy and joyful tone.
It's Ocean the sparkly unicorn.
Dexxy can only groan.

"I have lost my fire, Ocean.
It has disappeared, somehow.
I've repeatedly huffed and blown."
Dexxy's head is lower now.

"Oh Dexxy, this is so sad.
There must be something we can do.
Wait! I have a brilliant idea!
It's my time to help you."

"Follow me, now Dexxy,
There is someone you must meet."
So, she gets up to follow
With heavy, leaden feet.

Arriving at a cave,
Sparkling crystals all around,
A door creaks and opens.
Special magic has been found.

Standing there is a wizard
Who is dressed in sparkling blue.
"Oh welcome, Dragon Dexxy.
Now, what can I do for you?"

Dexxy tells the mystery
Of her fire that is no more.
The wizard presents a book.
Inside, there are spells galore.

"First we need some elements.
On Dexxy, all will be poured.
We need LOVE, JOY, and BELIEF
To discover our reward."

Ocean knows what her gift is.
She gives JOY straight away.
Squirrel Family hears the news
And gives BELIEF to save the day.

"What is left," the wizard said,
"But Love to make Dexxy strong."
Wilbur the Walrus is next
His bright LOVE rights every wrong.

"The spell is complete, dear Dexxy.
Your friends have helped you now.
You've done so much for them-"
Then they hear a soft "meow".

"Dexxy, please could you help me?"
Says Little Cosmo cat.
"My paws have frozen up."
Dexxy gives him a gentle pat.

"Dexxy you can do this
We all believe in you!"
Suddenly the flames appear
And the ice melts right through!

In Dexxy's relief so sweet,
She remembered Pearl, her friend.
Away she flew to save the day,
On Dexxy you can depend.

Pearl, with her bike still tied,
Struggles to break it free.
Dexxy said,"I have returned!"
And she burns the rope, quickly.

Dexxy the mystical dragon,
The creature we most admire,
Helps her friends out of trouble,
And they help regain her fire!

Gemma Bond, author of 'Dexxy the Determined Dragon', loves nothing more than to devise stories from her crazy imagination and Baye (her daughter) always plays a big part during the story creating process.

Living in Buckinghamshire (UK) as a single parent, author, hair artist, empath and reiki practitioner- Gemma loves helping others, being social and embarking on new challenges.

She loves nothing more than taking her daughter to exciting new places, from fairy festivals to surfing at the most beautiful beaches - adventuring and being in nature.

At their family home they have two beautiful pets - Alonso their 14 year old cat and Clover their crazy golden retriever.

Both Gemma and her daughter Baye have a "wicked" sense of humour, they both find fun in pretty much anything they do and there is NEVER a dull moment.

Gemma hope's to empower children to build resilience, inner strength and determination. Inspiring all children to see the magic in the world and breed general kindness - positivity amongst everyone.

Jo Blake illustrator/artist, lives in Devon with her family and much loved dog 'Blue'. When she isn't in her art studio, she is gaming, watching retro cartoons and being in the beautiful countryside.

Printed in Poland
by Amazon Fulfillment
Poland Sp. z o.o., Wrocław